Puppy Love

By Wayne Carley EC

Drawings by Erica Merkling

GARRARD PUBLISHING COMPANY
CHAMPAIGN, ILLINOIS

Puppy Love

Leslie wanted a puppy.
She wanted a puppy very much.
One day her father said,
"I have two things
for you."

"Is one a puppy?"
Leslie asked.
"Come and see,"
her father answered.

"We have
a baby brother for you."
"I don't want a baby brother,"
said Leslie.

"Come and see him,"
her father said.
"Here's your baby brother,"
said Leslie's mother.
"His name is Jimmy."

He was small.
He had a red face.
He was crying.
"I don't like him,"
said Leslie.

"Here's something else,"
said Leslie's father.
It was a puppy!
He was small.
He was black and white.
He had a happy face.
"Oh!" said Leslie.
"Thank you, thank you!

May I hold him?"
"Here he is,"
said Leslie's father.
"But be careful.
He's very little."

Leslie held her puppy.

He was soft.

He was warm.

He licked her face.

"What will you name him?"
asked Leslie's mother.
Leslie looked at her puppy.
The puppy licked
her face again.

"I'll call him Lickins,"
she said.
"He likes to lick my face."
Leslie went outside
to play with her new puppy.

For the next few weeks,
Leslie was very busy.
She had a lot to do
to take care of Lickins.

One day her mother said,
"I'm going to give
the baby a bath.
Would you like to help?"
"No," said Leslie.
"I have to brush Lickins."

Another day, her mother said,
"I'm going to feed Jimmy.
Won't you help me?"
"No," said Leslie.
"I'm going to feed Lickins."

It wasn't long
before Lickins started to grow.
So did Leslie's baby brother.

Soon Leslie's mother said,
"Jimmy can sit up."
"Not as well as Lickins can,"
said Leslie.

She made Lickins
sit up and beg.

One morning Leslie's mother
had a cold
and stayed in bed.
She called to Leslie,
"I want you
to look after Jimmy today."

"I don't know
how to look after him,"
said Leslie.

"Just keep him happy,"
her mother said.
"But how?" asked Leslie.
"The same way
you keep Lickins happy,"
her mother answered.
"Now, off you go.
I'll be here if you need me."
Leslie went into Jimmy's room.
When he saw Leslie,
he began to cry.
"Shhh," said Leslie,
"do you want your toy?"
She gave the baby his toy.

He threw it on the floor,
and he cried harder.
Just then, Lickins
came into the room.
He heard the baby crying.
So he began to cry too.

Leslie knew what to do.
She patted Lickins and said,
"There, there,
don't cry, little Lickins."
Lickins stopped crying.

But Jimmy cried and cried.
Leslie patted the baby
and said, "There, there,
don't cry, Jimmy."
The baby stopped crying.

Lickins got his ball.
He wanted to play.

Leslie rolled the ball
across the room.
Lickins ran after it.
He brought it back.

The baby laughed.
He wanted to play too.
Leslie put a blanket
on the floor.

She put the baby
on the blanket.
Then she got
the baby's toy
and gave it to him.
Jimmy held it up
and laughed.

Leslie played with Lickins
and with Jimmy
for a long time.
Lickins was tired
and lay down.

"You're tired," she said.

"It's time you go to sleep."

She sat down

and held Lickins.

Lickins fell fast asleep.

Jimmy was tired too.
Leslie picked him up
and held him.
"You're tired too," she said.
The baby also fell asleep.

Leslie's mother
came into the room.
Leslie was holding
the sleeping puppy
and the sleeping baby.

Leslie's mother
put Jimmy in his bed.
Then she picked up Lickins.
She put him
on the blanket.

Leslie and her mother
went out of the room.
"You did a good job, Leslie,"
said her mother.

"Oh, it wasn't so hard,"
said Leslie.
"Lickins and Jimmy
are both babies.
They both like to play.
They both like to sleep.

They're very much alike,
except one has fur
and one doesn't!"

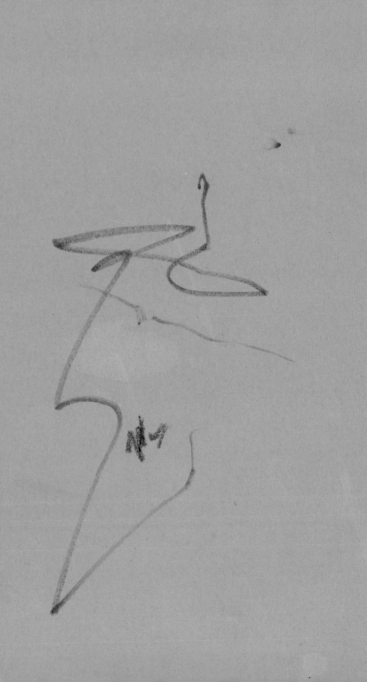